GW00992138

# Walking into a Pub in Glasgow

Michael D M Mhike

Copyright © 2012 Michael D M Mhike

All rights reserved.

ISBN:1530554292
ISBN-13:9781530554294

## DEDICATION

I dedicate this book to people interested in Glasgow social life, and its dynamic position over the years to present, gathered through information gotten from patrons from Glasgow's local pubs and the surroundings.

# CONTENTS

Acknowledgments      I

1   What you see is what you get      1

2   Billy integrates and later receives eviction order      4

3   Patron Victoria's beauty causes commotion in pub      7

4   Billy meets Denver      10

5   A woman in Royal Stuart Tartan approaches Billy for business in pub      13

6   Evil Gold diggers      16

7   Grounds breaking experiences      20

8   Hellas's dramatic showdown      22

9   Billy's melancholy      25

10   Billy is liberated from prison, encounters Denver and loses his laptop and four wrist watches from the hotel room.      27

.

## ACKNOWLEDGMENTS

I acknowledge friends like **Dereck Coyle** and others whom I encountered in a city pub in Glasgow and gave me the title for this book. Also, **Margret Sweeney** showed interest by buying my first book and encouraged me to adept to authoring this book. The following individuals are to be remembered for giving me the spiritual orgasm to build faith of success namely, **Stephen Scott** and his wife **Norah.**

# 1 WHAT YOU SEE IS WHAT YOU GET

Billy had just come from College to arrive at his flat and made himself something to eat and left his flat to approach a local pub for the first time. He is a foreigner coming from overseas and knew nobody living nearby his flat. He is a nice cool gentleman who likes to learn things. He respects people regardless of what color or creed they are and likes to treat everyone the same.

It's a Friday night and there is a Karaoke at a local pub and he took a little walk, about five minutes and got to the local pub called Silver-Back. He walked straight to the counter and asked the bartender for a pint of lager. He took his pint of lager and sat down next to two old ladies who sat with two men of middle age.

Sitting overture was a rectangle shape with an opening on the near side to the bar for easy access. One of the gentleman sitting with old ladies beckoned at Billy and listen to what he said;
"Hi pal are you lost?" the gentleman asked his face looking as if he is highly sunken.
"No not all" Billy replied somberly
"So why are you here?" asked the gentleman.
Billy hesitated to reply this gentleman and looked him into his eyes and replied, "Excuse me mate, I thought this was a pub for everyone which is why I came to socialize and listen to Karaoke".
Then another lady sitting next to the gentleman raised her head to ask Billy a question, "Can you sing?" asked the lady
"Yes of course I can sing "answered Billy.
"Which song are you going to give us?" asked the lady
"I have a dream by ABBA" Billy replied
"Sorry what's your name"? repeated the Lady
"Billy" Billy replied

At this moment the gentleman was quiet and busy chatting with his other gentleman.

"Would you like me to go and put the request for you" said the lady "Yes of course if it's possible I'm ready anytime madam" replied Billy.

Remember this was the first time Billy walked into his local pub, so you could imagine how it feels for a sudden challenge like confusion like encounter. Obviously, the gentlemen posed a very nasty question to Billy, the one about why you are here. However, Billy was a reasonable person, he understood that some humans have respect for others while some humans have not, let alone under the influence of alcohol, or perhaps it makes sense to say the amount of alcohol and the type of alcohol consumed does affect human behavior at times

Billy was thoughtful, by using a tactful idea of singing at Karaoke people would know him that now he is part of the community, and other to use as a token of integration. Billy was not a very good Karaoke singer but had to do it to achieve this goal.

His turn came, and his name was called and was handed the mic by the DJ. He sang "I have a Dream" from ABBA group.

When he stood up everyone cheered because it was a surprise to the local patrons as they had never seen someone of color offering to sing or even entering a pub like this to socialize or drink. Billy sang the song with a little bit of nervousness although the lady DJ sang along with him to give him confidence. The resultant performance was just so good.

Thus, how Billy became known and accepted by members of this local pub. They started to ask him with respect and some even offering him lagers especially that lady who booked his name down for a song.

The local pubs around Billy's new residence had a kind of a tradition which he noticed, it is that when you walk into any pub in Glasgow you have got to have six pounds to buy yourself a drink and spare coins to buy a friend. It contradicts with another tradition that a man enters a pub where he is well known and buys a dark lager for example john smiths but watches himself when it's about to finish. Before it finishes, he lifts it up and looks through the bottom of his glass to see who is going to buy the next round. This sounded like a joke to Billy not until he was told by one local patron who had tried to be his friend by talking about Africa that he had been there couple of years back but still could not remember the name of the country he visited there when he was soldiering under the commonwealth banner

In fact, there was no subject to be chatted about regards Africa, but this ironically could mean that this patron talking to Billy was a pretender as if to like him yet only perplexed that he was not used to sharing a pub with people of other cultures. The patron I shall name as X showed uneasiness when speaking to Billy as this could be noticed by the way he would intone a question to Billy, "I don't mean to be racist, but can I ask you a question if you don't mind me asking" X asks. Yes, replied Billy. "What brings you here? And why Glasgow of all the places? Have you no got places to visit there in Africa? Or elsewhere askes X.

This shows that if it's a one-off question from one patron it is accepted and not when it becomes the same question every pub you enter in Glasgow only to be met with the same question for ten years. Does this mean certain cultures are welcome while others are not welcome in Glasgow? These questions have remained unanswered for ten years to Billy or anyone of other cultural background. This is annoying because in this 21st century people must learn to accept other cultures so by working together they share different skills and could boost the country economy through improved technologies and global policies. Even in the national events all cultures should be involved together be it sports, business and politics. It is said "every little help's" and so can it be also said "every culture helps". this goes without mentioning the fact that only referring to people of sense willing to amalgamate peacefully and display social norms and values at real time expertise. The world could be improved that way. Billy is in traumatic state of mind because he never gets what he asks for.

## 2 BILLY INTERGRATES AND LATER RECEIVES EVICTION ORDER

Billy Goma was still awaiting his appeal results from the Home office while he was given a house while waiting. He was so stressed wondering when his leave to remain in the country shall come. This is so because this was the third time Billy had received accommodation and taken away from him. He set his time to wait in the following manner, that during business days he would rather be taking up a course of some sort to keep himself out of trouble.

He joined the local community meetings which would need to be attended twice a month. The purpose of the meetings was to discuss problems that may be facing the community in conjunction with the district council and the police. Effects like drug abuse, antisocial behavior were among other things discussed at this meeting. Billy was the only man of other culture and it was the first time this has historically happened. The total number of the group ranged between six and nine excluding the councilor and the two police officers who attended. The group was code named the councilors who voted among themselves to become community councilors.

It means these councilors were resident to this very district which conducted these meetings on a fortnightly basis. Billy enjoyed being part of the group, but the question one would ask is, was Billy's presence making any difference? No, it did not make any difference, as Billy was only an attendee without contributing anything because each time in this meeting when he tried to suggest something, it was not taken seriously one because his English accent would not be understood properly and therefore they would be no confirmation to what he said but just silence to allow him to mumble according to the rest of the group. Little did Billy know that he was accepted into this council meeting to satisfy the community that they were integrated and to ratify the awareness that the presence of ever increasing number of foreigners is in the community. How long does it take people to accept people of other cultures into their society? This seem to be everywhere on the planet, but it depends which side of the planet will you be standing. Billy tried to invite some members from his culture and for other cultures to come and join him at the council meetings, but they were scared. A member of other culture was attacked, and his legs broken, and wallet snatched, and he was left to die until a good Samaritan called the ambulance to come and rescue him in this very council district and it was during daylight at a corner of the flats as he was coming from the shops.

Another scenario is that Billy used to visit the local Councilor living about fifty meters away from his flat. His sitting room was always full of smoke like a chimney why because he liked to smoke the Harsh one rollup after another. He only became a councilor because he was the longest survivor in this district council. It was learnt that his father left him this house before he passed away. Communal people understood him very well, but they could do nothing to change his habit of smoking harsh. Sometimes it is a good idea to live with people the way they are and to adjust yourself to their level when you encounter them. This is the way it is in some societies hence a strange phenomenon to others.

Billy would go together with his community council members for a drink after the council meetings but did not like it when an intruder just appeared to our group and hit the hell out of our local councilor that we had to intervene to serve his live. No explanation as to why this happened either from the victim or any member of the group. Grapevine news said the councilor was beaten because he had not paid for his harsh to someone. Billy found this kind of societal viral to him that he wished he could be changed to a better community but had no means to do so because he had no recourse to public funds which could have enabled him to change and rent in another location. Billy had stayed in this locality for almost nine months and had made some friendship in this community.

He received bad news from the authorities that his appeal had failed and so he had to leave his flat in the next six months and during this time he would not be having any financial benefit from nowhere.

This left Billy a desperate man. He had a girlfriend but the sooner the news reached the fiancés ears, that was end of the relationship. She moved on with her life without Billy. His own friends no longer allowed him to come to their house for the simple reason that they were not able to give him help. During the six-month grace period to leave the house Billy could go to the food banks timeously to get some groceries for himself.

The final day to vacate his house arrived when Billy had no idea as to where he would be next. A friend of his culture had mercy on him and called him to his house. Billy left everything that was in the house beds electrical gadgets tv and clothes. Billy took his medium sized sachet put as much as could fit and went to his friend who lived about twenty-minutes' walk from his flat. The problem with his new friend was that he was an alcoholic who did not allow to be shot of beer at any given time and has never allowed himself for a single day except when he is going to sign at the job center. This was a difficult scale for Billy to adjust to. He had to do what the Romans do. Billy himself is a nice man well educated and likes a good life or a trouble-free life. One would wonder what next about Billy coping up with an alcoholic.

However, Billy devised himself a timetable to be away from home which was either going to the library or going to the food bank each morning. It worked only a few days but stress overweighed Billy that he indulged into drinking alcohol. Billy was diabetic, so he had to watch what to eat especially in the morning. No, it could not happen diet control as well for some time to come.

## 3 PATRON VICTORIA'S BEAUTY CAUSES COMMOTION IN PUB

This is a song of every Glaswegian when they meet someone of unusual background to them in any pub in Glasgow. Billy notices that in each pub he walks into, it is rare to leave the pub without being asked this question. He had to have the same answer anyway, that he came to Glasgow because the people are friendly, it's cheaper to leave in it and lastly that he ran away from persecution from his original country.

What an experience for Billy for almost ten years he has lived in this city same question hence a song. What would any reader think of under Billy's situation? Would any reader be glad to be always reminded that he or she is not a Glaswegian even under peak of social happiness? Billy adapted to know that he is indirectly unwelcome in Glasgow, but because he just wanted to carry on with life like any other human being. Billy was already depressed with his status being an asylum seeker and went to the pub to socialize and to feel accepted. One cannot force people to like you if you are of other culture in Glasgow general. Was it a road to neverland? Or a road to Hell.

Billy was in another pub where he was confronted with a beautiful mature single lady. She asked Billy to join her for some drinks. A lad approached from the back of the pair and whispered to the accompanied lady that "I am just going to the bank ATM and I will be right back in five minutes". whispered the intruder a lad. Billy just kept his head down and carried on exchanging the conversation with the lady. In brief the lady whose name had introduced herself as Victoria, warned Billy that "that man who was talking behind me wants to change our situation" said Victoria.

"How" Billy inquired.

"Snatching me from you but I said that I am with someone" Replies Victoria.

His behavior was not fair to us, has was disrespectful to you, just because you are of other cultures "replied Victoria.

"Well', replied Billy,' it's one of those things, I am not really bothered if you deal with him" mentioned Billy.

There was silence for a few seconds and the conversation went on as normal. No sooner had Billy and Victoria stated enjoying talking to each other than the lad intervened back from the ATM.

"Victoria what drink can I get you", said the lad.

"I am sorry I am having one already from Billy", Victoria replied to the lad.

"Can I please have a short word with you Victoria", the lad demanded with his face fool of jealous and ignorance.

Victoria had to excuse herself from Billy as the lad muscled out Victoria to go to sit next to him in the same pub. Billy kept cool and went on enjoying his drink. Billy changed the sitting position, he went to the dancehall where there was sitting plan intended for everyone and was most popular with the 50's and 60's old's. There is always a DJ entertainer with relevant music for his patrons. This day he played hip hop and reggae vibes. Billy joined others in dancing hip hop. It was fantastic experience for Billy.

While Billy enjoyed socialization in this new discovery, guess who approached him? It was Victoria and she immediately jumped onto Billy's waist and crossed her legs hanging her arms on top of Billy's shoulders as if she was an infant clinching onto her mothers' back. What a surprise that was for Billy who had literally forgotten about Victoria since she was last seized by that lad. Victoria apologized to Billy for being a while with the lad. She said she was scared not to go to that lad saying that its typical of Scottish man to shun every Scotswoman if she appears with other cultures in their territory. This is instinct, it happens to every culture jealous hate. Victoria mentioned that the man was so unsocial on their encounter and the bar tenders had to call the Police to excuse him from the bar and he was also barred from that bar.

"Good for him" Billy replied Victoria. After physically browsing Billy, Victoria joined him for the drink although she sounded a bit tipsy. They were happier together and performed some good dance on the stage with others.

The couple were up until the club was closed. They went separate ways even though the lady wanted Billy to come with him to her house that night. After what happened before they settled scarred Billy to ever take any chance for an after party at Victoria's nor to even be accompanied by her to his friend's house. They exchanged numbers and were to rearrange to meet again.

That must have been very cruel of Billy as Victoria had obsession to him. I suppose she also needed security of a man that night for consolation and love. This was a stalemate situation. All because of a psychopathic lad who coincided with them in this local pub who spared a little drama with Victoria. The problem was that Billy could not take risk of challenging local resident in their local resident bar. He had to exercise extreme caution when it comes to these things especially when alcohol is involved.

Victoria was sharing a house with her son who had also invited a girlfriend to stay there. She was in good books with her son but did not like the son's girlfriend because she was alcoholic and into drugs.

## 4 BILLY MEETS DENVER

Billy walked into another pub in the central business district of Glasgow by a traditional Scotts name. It is near the central station. He encountered a group of patrons who were very friendly. They could chat to him and offer him something to drink. They would still ask him the question what brings him to Glasgow and where he is from? This is the time when Billy realized that it's a Scottish culture to ask people who they are and why they are here? It is this time Billy received these questions from some friendlier sources. Of course, this was in the city center and people look smart than they would look if they were in their village locations.

Suddenly there appears Denver a man of his color. Denver was a very chickee guy who always wanted people to listen to him only. Denver would not listen to anyone's conversation for more than ten seconds if he does nothing is going into his head. He was kind of a macho man who saw himself fit to lift an elephant. He took some asteroids to grow muscles so that he can show off to boys in the city. He was of middle age while Billy was of more mature age. Billy could accommodate him for two good reasons in public, one because they were of same color and they could communicate in their vernacular language and secondly, he was sort of an acquaintance. Denver would not be happy if someone buys him a drink in public and Billy was aware of that weakness. On this day Denver was show off with power to buy drinks because there were several females in the pub on who he had indicated he would love to have a conversation with.

Time passed as they went on discussing things about back home and how the people are surviving there. However, Billy wanted to call it a day, but Denver insisted on Billy to remain a little longer. He gave Billy an advance cash of thirty pounds which he would need back the following week. As is always in pubs when people meet for a drink they start talking softly and finally get to a heightened voice in fact shouting. There was music in this pub. Denver would not call any round after lending money to Billy which he was not prepared for. | That is the problem with Denver when he meets broke friends he takes advantage of them. They both new how to deal with each other.

Something happened, Billy told Denver he has had enough when he had only spent half the amount he borrowed from Denver, but Denver wanted to continue to drink. They argued seriously as friends and Denver then demanded his money back from Billy. That was a cruel intent from Denver, but like I described him before that's what Denver is made of and the whole community did not like him for that erratic behavior which is why even if Billy new him to exist, he would not be bothered to call him for a drink out. Denver had a bad previous life, he parted with his first wife after having had a child together and parted with the second wife after also having had a baby together. They all did not want to see him or even to give him access to see his children because of his bossy character. They were told to leave the pub by the security and the argument ensued outside until the police arrived. The police watched the drama at first, they said nothing watching from their cars. When Denver went towards Billy in a pretext to punch him, Billy pushed Denver back in anger where Denver fell on his back to the tar next to the police. Then the police took a move to arrest both and send them to the cells for that night. Billy regretted for allowing Denver into his life for once the previous day. Denver was a problem child. Denver was putting the problem of not being granted asylum to everybody. Maybe this was his way of drawing attention to the authorities that he needs resident status, done the wrong way. Denver had not ventured much into education, in fact he had not achieved any form of academic discipline in his life.

In fact, Denver wanted company with Billy because Billy was a most respectable, mature lad who was admired by all cultures he integrated with. Billy at some point was nominated a community leader and he even participated in social groups to refurbish football pitches and even helped paint a local church library. The only thing that did not make Billy right was lack of leave to remain in the United Kingdom. He was being housed after an appeal and one or three years later he was told to leave the house and start to make a fresh claim by the authorities. Billy was very resilient in trying to survive the destitution. He would go to colleges and asked permission to learn disciplines for example, pathways information technologies and business studies and many more. Billy was well known to every foodbank in the city. He had well-wishers who could help him with a few coins for bus pass and even to be invited to the local pub or city pub. Billy knew how to keep himself occupied as somebody who enjoys reading magazines and news from his country of origins. Billy is also learning to be a writer.

## 5 A WOMAN IN ROYAL TARTAN SKIRT APROACHES BILLY FOR BUSINESS IN PUB

When you have nothing to do in your house and you do not know when your decision from the Authorities is going to come, to say you now got your leave to remain in the country, one decides to do a lot of chores. Billy put on his favorite soap recorded while he is making up his bed and it's a bedroom seater and goes on to put his clothes into a washing machine and cleans his kitchen dishes. At sunset Billy decides where to go for a walk or heading for the city to socialize.

The later decision was his final answer because he had a few coins got after exchanging his voucher to cash. Billy preferred to go it alone and meet people himself as he was a sweet talker and a humorous person. He was talented to talk to people and one would wonder whether he prepared for the answers he gave, or it was his natural gift. He always made sure he would not meet Denver considering their previous encounter was not fruitful as they ended up in cell that other night. It was dawn and Billy had prepared and had his evening meal and ready to travel to town where he went to the west end of the city. He liked pubs in that area because they were rich and mature people patronizing those pubs. Karaoke was also available that night of a Saturday.

Billy took the bus no 61 and disembarked in the city, only to find out that the city was packed with clubbers that day because it was end of the month. He went into the Mud house just near the Glasgow Central Station. It is easy access to the bus station should he decide to go back home. He was greeted at the door by the doormen and allowed to enter. He met people to chat to after purchasing his pint of lager from the counter. Music was full blast that people had to speak up to communicate with each other. After one pint he settled with a nice gentleman who claimed to be from the outskirts of the city. They exchanged buying their drinks and going out for a smoke together. The gentleman introduced himself as Jim. Before they sat together Jim had asked a few questions about Billy whereabouts and whatnot as usual because Billy is of a different decent.

It was when Jim went to the counter to buy another round of drinks that Billy was approached by a beautiful Scotts woman dressed in Royal Stuart tartan skirt. She asked Billy, "Are you looking for business?" the woman asked.
"I have my own business in Seychelles which is being run by workers" flattered Billy.
" I mean tonight" said the woman displaying a chilled face. Seeing that Jim was approaching with the two pints of lager the woman walked away leaving Billy totally confused as he did not understand the woman story.

He told Jim what the woman was asking about from Billy. Before Billy had even finished to explain to Jim, Jim had burst into laughter with tears on his eyes. This left Billy even more perplexed like a judge unwilling to condemn his friend. After a few seconds of laughter which Billy had also joined in without clue Jim explained to Billy that the woman wanted sex for money. "Oh, thanks Jim, honestly I was lost" remarked Billy.
"So next time you know what it means when you are approached again" warned Jim.

This made a good night experience for Billy because he learnt some of the character traits found in the pubs and streets of Glasgow. Jim also said that these women are normally operating near the casinos and busy streets. He mentioned that they are not alone as they will have guys watching from a distance whom she secretly gives a signal when she hooks a prospect. He also mentioned that they are dangerous sometimes as they can rob you and way lay drunk people with money. Billy always wondered whether these women vying for business in the streets of Glasgow had chance to receive benefits or they already are? Are they serious or they want money to buy drugs which are so expensive that they cannot afford with their little benefits money. These questions remained unanswered to Billy. Billy did not pay rent or electricity on top of receiving a weekly voucher worth thirty-five pounds. This was Billy's advantage at the time because that's the situation when you are an immigrant claiming asylum before any decision is made whether to be granted leave to remain or not to be granted leave to remain in the United Kingdom.

Therefore, Billy always liked to socialize in Glasgow pubs in a move to make friends locally and integrate so that when his permission to remain in the United Kingdom is granted then it would become easier for him to forecast on social projects like working for charities. This was his great expectation. He was like hoping against hope as he developed depression at the same time he is waiting for the decision. Life is hard if one is walking a long journey and you don't know the destination. At least Billy had seized the opportunity of safeguarding a place at a college in the city which offered him a place. He has been schooling all the time he was housed. Even when Billy had no accommodation, he would continue going to college from night shelters or from temporary accommodation from friends. This is the complicated life Billy had to go through's the pub would be where he could experience night life after college. Sometimes he would go without money just to sing karaoke in his local pub and of course he would come out drunk most of the times like this because some fox liked him. On closure of the pub Billy would straddle back to his friends flat feeling a bit relaxed and happy alone and upon arriving at the flat, he would make himself a cup of decaffeinated tea or rooibos tea and tune smooth radio to make him sleep. As he was diabetic type two he would not forget to take his night tablet. He normally increased his night to the local pub especially weekends.

## 6 EVIL GOLD DIGGERS

Billy had stayed for a long time, about two and half years without making a steady partner. He started to chart with a girl who was his ex-girlfriend's bon-homie who had long left for overseas. Dolly was the name of his ex-girlfriend and Skala was the one whom Dolly had introduced to Billy, but Billy was hesitant to contact her for a long time until he was relocated a flat after submitting his fresh claims to the Authorities. She lived in Ireland couple of miles across the Irish seas.

One day Billy thought of contacting her through the social media and they clicked. Little did Billy Know that Skala had ultra-motive by agreeing to start a new relationship with her. Skala was also an immigrant to Ireland while she worked there. She was probably bored by living in a small island and wanted to come to the mainland Great Britain. However, before Billy talked to her, she had not even one friend in the mainland, so she was happy that Billy had accepted to move together with her. Billy had also thought that when Skala arrives, there would be some good odds for him to rely on Skala should his decision not become positive again when he would face eviction as is the case when you are a failed asylum seeker. A situation that both could not wait for, yet they arranged to meet in November 17th, 2015.
It was Billy who had to travel to Ireland to pick the girl-up as she had no idea of Scotland sponsored by Skala.

The chemistry of this relationship relied on the ultimate faith of both partners. It is said that it is right to do the right thing because it is right to be right and honest. Billy took this courage from a friend from the pub who had encouraged him to try and stay with a partner best of his color because they would understand each other better. Yes, Skala came from Africa and was African as well as Billy but were from neighboring states there in Africa as they were here too.

November comes, and Billy goes to board a ship to Ireland to fetch the new girlfriend to be, and that was Skala. It was two hours journey and Billy even communicated with his friends to let them know about how happy he was to procrastinate his new relationship. They were both right on time to meet and Skala looked calm and remained with an inquisitive face. They both retired briefly for a cup of coffee and a pint of Guinness for Billy. They partook their journey to Scotland and arrived safely at Billy's flat.

The next day Billy calls two of his friends who were also married to come to the flat and see his new partner. Of these two friends, one had leave to remain in the UK while the other Tara's had not yet been granted. Papiro, the guy with the leave to remain invited us both to go to the Local pub to introduce Skala to Glasgow life. There was some nice dance from Papiro and Skala after one round of drinks. Taras is the only one not drinking. This local pub was specially selected because it had cheap beers and spirits plus there was good music. What a fantastic moment for Billy and Skala and friends.

All along there was some exchange of numbers between Taras and Skala and even selfies were taken. Billy did not think there was anything wrong with Skala exchanging numbers with his two friends because he trusted them having lived together in the same locality for so many years. This is too good to be true a statement considering the shortcomings of their relationship.

The party was over and they all went to their homes living Billy and his new partner. They had not started any chemistry, yet as good things are worth waiting for. They had dinner of chicken tikka marsala prepared by Skala and it was lovely according to Billy. A call arrives on to Skala's handset set and guess where it was from? Taras liked Skala even though he had a wife at his flat in real-time. Taras was handsome looking guy that most men would never invite him when they are with their ladies. He has a charm that makes ladies to leave their men and run for him. It's like the harder they come is the harder they fall into situation with Taras.

After two minutes after talking to Taras, Skala said a statement that she is not intending to have intimacy with Billy as she had to decide on that? The news shocked Billy and he suddenly became uncomfortable with Skala. They argued and little bit but it was no sooner than they argued that Skala threatened to live really on the second day. She was drinking Captain Morgan Spice during this conversation and Billy was on his tennets lager.

She stood up and collected her suitcase and demanded to go. Billy was such a nice gentlemen and respects woman and is not a type to disappoint women. He was disappointed this time, that he opened the door for her to go out and she went, and Bill closed the door behind her. For one thing Billy suspected that she probably decided to go to guest houses and that his age is what he thought the girl could have changed her mind. Another most important thought was that since Skala knew that Billy have got no papers or leave to remain therefore would not satisfy her. Instead she cheated to love Billy for anyone else with money that she will come across.

Taras had achieved his diploma in plumbing but was not allowed to work as he was also waiting for his leave to remain in the United Kingdom. Taras had lots of money in his back pocket the day he came to meet Billy's new partner. He pulled out a bundle worth five thousand pounds. Billy was not surprised seeing him like that because he would do private plumbing to earn his leaving. Taras is the one who took Billy's girl that very second night when she said she is leaving, there was a taxi waiting outside for her to Tara's' flat as he had moved to stay to his wife's flat.

Billy was quite petrified with the occurrence of events as he was tipped by Papiro through a text, that the girl went with Taras. Papiro encouraged Billy to visits Taras Flat and he agreed, and they arrived. Papiros knocks the door and the door was answered by Lala who was Taras wife and a child girl. Billy followed in as the door was opened for them.

"Good evening and sorry to disturb you at this time of the night, 'Did you see Taras with another woman to day"? asks Billy disturbed.
 "Why uncle and who is she "asks Lala suspiciously.
"Because she is my friend but ran away with Taras" replied Billy angrily.
"Uncle step out of my door" Lala ordered Billy to leave.

Billy without hast stepped out and waited for Papiros to come out but in vain. After three minutes Billy walks back home about two miles away after midnight. An hour later Police arrives at Billy's flat and only asked if Billy ever saw Papiro that evening.

"Yes" answered Billy wondering.

They immediately handcuffed Billy and send him to the courts the following Monday.

Taras and Papiro had connived to dish Billy as a coverup to their snatching of his girlfriend and lied to the police that Billy wanted to rape his wife Lala. Papiro was on benefits so he would support everything said by Taras because he was making money on plumbing job. These were serious allegations, but Billy did not win it in court and therefore he was put on sex offenders register on top of a one-year sentence on social services.

When a dream is deferred sometimes a bewildering frustration and corroding bitterness ensues. Billy was hacked with the fourth evil in a man of good for the first time of his life. He felt neglected by the law and by everybody that he soon developed cancer and is diabetic and above all is still seeking asylum. One would wonder whether Billy got any life on this planet.

Billy had made such a great journey to cross the Irish seas only to get this mishap.

## 7 GROUNDS BREAKING EXPERIANCES

By the time Billy finished his sentence he had already been connected to a lady by Papiro. Her name as Hella was very sympathetic to what Billy had been through and was always with him all the time he would go to courts. Hella had an idea of the people who lend false accusations to Billy which is why she did not mind being on side of Billy. One thing that Hella knew about Billy was that Billy was a very intelligent boyfriend who could and always brought good changes to her life and the life of her disabled boy. She quite like the company of Billy as Billy was quite capable of fathering her mentally deranged boy.

Billy had no income at the time yet the help and refurbishments he did at Hellas's cottage was worth a fortune. It is said love is a blind devotion and this is true in Billy's contributions to Hella. He took Hella to places which no man had ever done in her life up to the age of fifty-four. These were places of interests like going to the camping, taking her and her son to Penzanze on summer holidays at their expenses though. Billy even bought a car for doing local shopping at nearby shopping malls. She really had a life changing experience with Billy. They could drive to big cities just for the weekend when the boy had been taken by his sister for the weekend. At times Billy did receive some small income from friends and churches he usually went to. This helped to center their financial relationship. Life looked good for the family.

Hella had her own health problems such as sporadic fissures especially after a drink. Billy had to be on guard always when they went out for a night a thing they were not quiet frequenting. The boy had learning disability, yet Billy wasn't bothered with it and Billy used to do most of the special dishes for dinners on weekend mostly. This had become a part of life for all but there was a little problem, when Hella wouldn't allow Billy to visit his friends of color at any given point, it was taboo at this new relationship. This disturbed Billy a bit, but he consented. Billy was not allowed to receive calls from sources unknown to Hella, if caught, big trouble. It was like Billy is in Prison as he had no choice, no money, and no accommodation elsewhere.

Billy was diagnosed with prostate cancer when he told Hella who did not mind about that. All she needed was company or partner for social standing. Hella was proper Glaswegian born and bred in Glasgow and had never travelled anywhere except to the caravan parks for fifty-four years. She is not the only one though in some places in Glasgow.

One day Billy, Mattock the boy, and Hella went out to the pub in Glasgow. They had buffet at a Chinese restaurant first and proceeded to the pub. There was Karaoke in this Scott bar as is always on Thursdays and Sundays. Hella was on desperado lager, Billy on Captain Morgan spice and coke while Mattock had McEwan's lager. They had first round, second round and on the third round Mattock gave them a son Sweet Caroline on the karaoke machine when his booked turn arrived. He sang wonderfully although with few mistakes to the song. Billy and Hella had gone to the stage for a dance to follow their son's song, Sweet Caroline. Eyes were on Billy's table as Billy was of color, yet it was difficult for anyone to approach Billy to ask him those obvious questions, "what brings you to Glasgow? "For the simple reason that Billy had a family.

Hella had kind of claustrophobia so she decided that they should leave either for home or for a much decent pub without Karaoke. Mattock argued with this point raised by Hella his mother, he wanted them to remain there for the enjoyed karaoke and it was his first time to venture in a pub as he wouldn't with his mum because they both need care every time they move out of the house. So, you could imagine Billy had so much to care for every minute of enjoyment or place outside home.

## 8 HELLA'S DRAMATIC SHOWDOWN

Billy is given a chance to go to the city to meet his friends. Billy spends a lot more time and arrives back home at midnight. Hella opens the door and shuts it again and locks it behind Billy. Hella who was lined up by Mattock at her back shouted through the glass that she will not allow him in tonight. Billy had nowhere to go as he was an asylum seeker waiting for his case to be decided upon by the Home Office. Billy's reaction was very calm as he was aware of the dangers of arguing with his partner. Billy went into his car parked in the backyard of the house to take a nap.

Hella was not pleased with the move Billy took, to sleep in his own car, so she called the cops for him. At this time Billy had lot of health issues and when the cops arrived Billy had wet trousers for staying too much outside the doors. The cops gave him a pillow to sit on at the back of the van and drove Billy to the nearest night shelter in the city. Night shelters are only open from eight o'clock in the evening to eight o'clock in the morning. Billy scrambled for the nearest public toilet which he got from the train station.

Billy took of his wet jeans and socked them in gent's toilet and rinsed them that he had to spend one hour in the gent's toilets to re wear his jeans. He was lucky because the hot drier was working in this gent's toilets to dry his jeans Remember Billy was driven to the city at around seven -thirty in the morning. He went to the nearest bookies to seek warmth and he stayed for almost two hours and then left for the national library. He was waiting for the night shelter to open, so he could go there to join other homeless guys. Slept one night at the shelter and the following day at midday Hella texted Billy to come back home. Billy doubted for a second because Hella was too possessive of Him and not helping Billy much and had stricter rules towards Billy because she knew Billy's weakest link.

Is it fair to take advantage of someone because he/she has no fixed aboard or even no income? What should be done to avoid such situations affecting the vulnerable people. At times such people are incriminated, raped, lied upon and lose all their possessions and everyone turns a blind eye to such people. It's like fun without fun. However, it goes without mentioning that people are treated differently from place to place and from country to country because of different norms and values in each society and different powers in each different society.

It did not take time for Billy to decide to respond to the text message Hella had sent him text by replying, "Yes I will be on my way honey". Hella and her disabled son Mattock both realized how important was the presence of Billy. He cut grass with lawn mower when the grass is tall, he took care of the bins. He was responsible for cooking as it was a suggestion from Billy to save income and the idea was welcomed by Hella. Hella was a chain smoker as she could finish forty cigarettes in a day. Billy had knowledge of IT, so he **was** handy to fix adapters, link internet to Phones. Billy also encouraged quick bill respond so they won't slag behind or accrue unpaid bills at end of each month.

Mattock was hilarious guy, he was accepting everyone on his WhatsApp and Facebook requests. It's when he received a call from China that alerted Hella the mother and when she intoned to Mattock, "who are you talking to? "asked Hella.

"Mum it's my friend from China", replied Mattock.

"Delete them, in fact give me the phone, I will delete them myself", demanded Hella.

"Oh no mum", cried Mattock handing the phone over to her mum.

The truth of the matter is that Mattock had a learning disability. He is someone who has no clue on how to work a smart phone. The only thing he would remember was to receive a call and to call. Billy had to spend much time impacting knowledge to his step son Mattock. Mattock had improved in understanding some smart phone applications. His problem was his memory lost some stuffs.

A week after reconciliation Hella and Billy and Mattock decided to go out to a local pub. Hella had received her back pay of some living out allowance as she was not in a council house but a rented house. The night went out well and they all took one taxi to bring them home. Billy prepared the meal for everyone and the enjoyed their meal and they retired to bed.

Hella and Billy always had a bottle of Captain Morgan spiced. Billy put on his pajamas while Hella was still in the kitchen. Billy was on his bed now enjoying a tot of Captain Morgan Spice. When Hella came to the bedroom she had her glass on side of bed prepared by Billy. They finished Captain Morgan Spice and coke a tot each. Billy said he would not mind having the second tot where Hella said she was fine she could not take anymore.

Drama clicked in when Billy took to drinking the second tot. Hella told Billy not to take another one but Billy did. Hella just went out of the blankets ducked downstairs. She was going to call the police secretly and its true, the next thing Billy is approached by a cop while in bed and when he asked the cop why he was in this bedroom Bill was apprehended for breach instantly uplifted to cell with his pajamas and without his wallet and watch. One can imagine how Hella did not care for Billy, but was selfish, a woman who just needed what she wants no matter how it takes. The scenario is that Hella had stayed for almost thirty years without a partner. When she got Billy, her character started to unleash bit by bit and the unfortunate partner became Billy of all that ever wanted to go out with her. Hella had also two estranged daughters, but one was brought back into the family by Billy and Hella after discussing. The help Billy was giving or being given was tormenting. Now he is in cell, it's a Friday evening meaning that he is to see ousting on Monday for silly reason. The question is could the cop not stop to think it's a fake report, or could the cop even though devolved powers discreet the crime reporters? It is easy to say there is a special reason why cop is tough to the north of the border or are we walking out of a pub in Glasgow. Balance should be struck between respect for foreigners who are implicated as crime doers and the police understanding and acceptance of the need for proper and fair integration of people living in one society as one civilized folk.

## 9 BILLY'S MELANCHOLY

On a Monday following a cast into the cell, Billy was given a bail on breach of peace. He had immediately become homeless and therefore the judge had no option but to send Billy to the remand prison. Plea was not given yet to allow further investigations. There was an option given to Billy to phone somebody who would accept to give him an address but in vain through the help of the Social Services but still to no avail. Telephone numbers given were not answered by his reliable friends.

It was a moment of sadness, melancholy and depression for Billy, it was going to be the first time in life to be issued with a prison number hence the blues holiday. He had just been from prostate cancer operation that he had incontinence as is always with post prostate gland removal. The prison officials were very helpful by providing the incontinence pads to him as well as his diabetic tablets. He was still on his pajamas that other inmates were laughing at him. Billy is a very friendly person and it did not take him a day to make friends. He put a request for his wallet to be brought to prison through social services. When he left his wallet, there was eighty pounds in it but only to find there was twenty pounds only in it. Hella had obviously helped herself to sixty pounds as she was a chain smoker. That was taking advantage of Billy by using the police platform who she had already brain washed and using the out of sight mentality.

When the going gets tough, the tough gets going. Billy embarked on prison education offered to every inmate interested in studying. He took up business studies, anger management course and marketing courses while in prison for that short period of remand he was there. Billy fought many situations in his life all because he has no leave to remain paper. He spent one month and half and had two courts attendance of which he was liberated on the second month. He impressed the Prison teachers as he was keen to learn and probably some of the material in marketing was revision to him.

Other spare time he participated in gym and morning walks carefully as his op was still fresh. Billy's thought sometimes was disturbed as in really sense this was not his worth to suffer from losing his freedom. It was a momentous and unparalleled occasion of entering prison. This was not a good stop, a prison because he had never been and more so just for having no fixed aboard. What a crossroad of shattered dreams he imagined as he did walks.

Billy met lots of inmates during class lessons who were there for various crimes. However, the situation looked not very bad because the food was good for a start and each individual inmate had had own cell with tv flask and a single bed and ensuite. All he needed was times for work up and position of the washing machine and kitchen outside rooms.
Billy made friends with Redpath because Redpath vowed to allow Billy to come and share his cottage after he is released. They exchanged phone numbers and Billy was given a winter jacket to wear while in, because he came with pajamas only. This was a good but not easy situation for Billy. He earned two pounds each day he went for either exercises or lessons. He would be able to buy his tobacco and, he had remainder of the twenty pounds from his wallet which was brought in by the social services from Hella. He could make one call a day from a phone booth inside the prison complex. Its sad because never got an answer from his friends. They put their phones on voice mail that Billy ended up forgetting about trying to contact his friends while in prison.

Some inmates showed high blood pressure of deceptive, rhetoric and an anemia of concrete performance, an experience unavoidable of places like this. Schizophrenia a corrosive evil could be noticed from some inmates who would end up with guided missiles and misguided men if the wall of the prison were to be removed. Billy felt his dreams deferred as this was leading to his bewildering frustration and corroding bitterness. All the time he felt he was homeless even if here, or even yonder. He would not trust his offer from Redpath of accommodation because Redpath was a goal bird. He only liked Billy because they played chess together. Billy had

two days left to attend court and possibly be liberated. He wished his inmates happy new year as it was also approaching.

## 10 BILLY IS LIBERATED FROM PRISON, ENCOUNTERS DENVER AND LOSES HIS LAPTOP AND FOUR WRIST WATCHES FROM THE HOTEL ROOM.

On Friday morning, Billy was liberated, and a hotel was arranged for him for three weeks by the grace of social services. This time is to allow Billy to sort out his accommodation problems since his partner Hella had split with him. How was this going to be possible when Billy had no recourse to public funds? The social department worked with appropriate department to make sure that he gets the accommodation he needs as Billy was an ill person in terms of post cancer operation and other serious health problems he had.

Billy believed that this could be the end of his destitution and hope sooner he will be accommodated. Is there something that Billy needs to know about getting housed? He had been in diaspora for almost ten years where he would be housed for between six months to three years and then kicked out within those ten years. The main reason for this was the fact that his asylum case would have been decided negatively and it has become a trend In Billy's diasporic and diabolic life. He is also catching up with age and nothing has happened yet except perusing his health status. If walls had ears, Billy's sufferings would be comforted. He would have a sanctuary, hope and aspiration for his life. Billy would be able to go back to his country and attend funerals for his clan dying of hunger war and diseases. Billy cannot even afford to renew his passport or go back to his home as he is skin, or a rolling stone that gathers no mass. Billy's faith is what keeps him alive, that everything has got an end. He believes that one day wright shall be right because he feels it right to be right and honest based on his faith. He believes that all his health and accommodations problems shall turn into air history.

Billy is at the hotel for almost a week now also waiting for the results of his accommodation. He receives a call from Denver his old friend. Denver intends to come to the hotel and see Billy and to give him some bit of cash to survive on while at the hotel. They both agree to meet at a pub In Glasgow. Apparently, this pub was frequented by young millionaires little did Bill know, only Denver knew as he called them close friends.

Billy arrived at this pub and meets Denver. Denver had a chat with Billy and handed Billy with a twenty-pound note to keep in his pocket and he was unhappy of the fact that Hella, Billy's partner had behaved in such atrocious manner which landed Billy in free holiday in prison. Billy's is introduced to a self-proclaiming young millionaire in this high-class pub in the west end of the city. The millionaire called Billy to come closer and handed Billy with forty pounds also to put in his pocket as they all were told about his situation by Denver.

The whole table of three guys was loaded on top with expensive champagnes, Jack Daniels, Captain Morgan spice etc. you name it. Billy did not quite like meeting such young man in the state which they were already, drunk, talkative and arguing at loud voices. Billy did not know whether to leave Denver with these new friends or not. Billy decided to just chill out with these guys as the pub looked nice and most patrons were descent people.

Denver decides to go to the hotel with Billy. Billy had not quite learnt about terms and conditions of inviting a friend to the hotel. They left the millionaire and his friend still drinking and chanting. It was a good night for Billy at least he got some intoxication from the pub had a nice drink.where he saw the millionaire. Hey, they both were highly unsuck. What happens at the hotel is that they both went to hotel pub and

There is something that always bothered Billy about Denver, that he was just his acquaintance but would not normally spend the whole night with because Denver was not a trusted boy. Denver had also not fixed aboard but he managed to stay with girlfriends because he is of a younger age compared to Billy who was twice as old. Denver would not accept it if Billy gets accommodation before him. So, he was quite nosey and destructive to Bills life on this encounter.

Denver stared to behave in an unprecedented manner at this hotel. Chatting loud and claiming to be a finer person than Billy. They slept in the room one on couch and Billy on bed. Billy had valuables in the same room he trusted his old pal to enter. Denver had a hidden tag and was not honest or perhaps he just got too drunk and stole Billy's laptop and four wrist watches and disappeared during night after Billy had passed out in his sleeping, innocently drunk.

## ABOUT THE AUTHOR

Michael Donaldson Makumucha Mhike is a Great Zimbabwe born writer. Born in 1958 he was the last in a family of eight. He arrived in Great Britain on January 22nd, 2005 on a business trip but never went back due to the unsettled nature in Zimbabwe which carried on for some years.

This second edition follows his first book "My Life in Africa" published in 2017 while he lived in Scotland. The writer has moved to England now to join his nephew who runs a charity organization in Manchester and worldwide.